THE COUNTING

EVAN SHAPIRO

Start

'Are you ready for next week?' Jones asks as we rattle along on the intercity SkyCar. The carriage jolts to a stop mid-station.

'I hate when it does this,' he says. 'I feel like we're going to be here all day. Makes me anxious.' He looks nervously over my shoulder and out the window to the cityscape.

'I know,' I reply. I hate it too, but not because we are hanging precariously in the sky. I just want to get to the office and secure my favourite spot in the open plan before an ignorant newbie takes it.

They call my workplace agile. I have the 'freedom' to sit where I like, to hot desk. One day happily in the southwest corner with a view of the city, the following day stuck in the airless, windowless wasteland next to the men's room. I can go to a designated private space to make phone calls, or use meeting rooms when I must. But they don't encourage meetings. If you have too many meetings, they think you're not working enough. So, we have quiet and quick conversations instead of meetings. I don't mind that too much. I don't like meetings. I always end up with a to-do list after a meeting and a deadline for the to-do list. And less time to meet the deadline of the to-do list. And someone is always counting our time and comparing it to our to-do lists.

'Are you ready then?' Jones asks again. I know it's only once a year, but if you aren't ready you could miss the deadline, or worse, starve from lack of supplies. 'You know nothing's open. You can't afford robo delivery for every meal? Can you?'

'I'm ready, Jones,' I reply. 'When have you ever known me not to be ready? I've got a week's supply of food.'

'I know, I know. You are Mr Planning. I guess I'm talking to myself. I'm making two big meals,' Jones says. 'That way I don't have to count more. It's just two. I'll put one in the fridge and the other into separate containers in the freezer and just heat them when I need them.'

'If they are in separate containers, you'll need to count them?'

'Damn, you're right,' Jones says. 'There's no escape is there?'

'I'm going in hard this year, three maybe four days max. Finish the count as quickly as possible, and then take the rest of the week to myself.'

'That and find the Holy Grail,' Jones says. 'I've tried that,' Jones continues. 'Never works for me. I only ever scrape in under the deadline.'

'You've got too much stuff then?'

'Don't say that?' Jones refutes, looking at me to lower my voice. 'Don't say that word.'

'Stuff?' I say.

'Shush,' he says and uses his hand as if pushing the word down.

'It's not illegal to have stuff, Jones. It's just illegal to have too much stuff.

'Yes, you idiot,' Jones says. 'That's what you just accused me of.' He looks nervously around the crowded SkyCar carriage. 'In public! But it's not true,' his voice slightly raised to ensure anyone listening will hear. 'I purged only two months ago and I'm well within approved ratios.' He looks around again. No one seems to care.

'Well good for you. Should be an easy count then.'

'Yes, but I really thought I was onto something with the frozen meals. Damn containers.'

'You have to count everything, Jones. Everything. And 'The Collective' wants you to observe, Jones. You need to be aware of what you have and the impact it has on your life. On all our lives.'

He looks me in the eye and without saying a word I can tell he thinks I'm full of shit. We both know the rules of the count. Repeating them out loud just means you are reminding yourself not to break them.

The SkyCar carriage lurches forward and we move again. I glance at my watch. I'm on schedule to make the office in time to claim my spot, but it will be tight.

'How's your BMI?' I ask.

'You can't ask me that here!' He looks over his shoulder again.

'Why not?' I ask. 'Everyone needs to control their BMI. It's fundamental to rewards and benefits.'

'Which is why you can't fucking ask me that in the middle of a fucking SkyCar carriage,' he snaps.

'Like these phone zombies care, Jones. Look I just insulted all of them and they don't even look up to defend themselves. You and I, my friend, are the only two humans without plugs in our ears, the only ones conversing. Did you notice that?'

'Fine,' Jones says, calming himself. He closes his eyes for a second and I can see he's doing a micro TransMed to deal with our conversation.

'Are you taking MatzaBurn?' I push more for the fun of it, expecting the mention of weight loss pills will challenge him further and elicit another snappy comment.

'Yes, and it's working,' he replies. He's learning not to bite. Damn.

'You will be fine for the end of count weigh-in then. Don't worry so much,' I say and place a reassuring hand on his shoulder. 'You look well, so there is that.' I extract a reluctant smile from Jones as our bodies shift with the movement of the carriage.

The SkyCar pulls into our station. We both know that as soon as the doors open we'll be parting ways. We know what it takes to get our favourite spots and a slow meandering from the station to the office, chatting happily, is not the answer. No, as soon as the doors of the SkyCar open on the platform, it will be dog eat dog. At least half of the phone zombies will lower their screens and focus on the mission at hand. Everyone for themselves in the pursuit of the best positioned hot desk. There will be plenty of time for talk at meal break or when the end of day whistle blows. Then we can take our time, converse idly as we are sandwiched in with the crowds all making their way home. The shuffling living dead transfixed on their screens. Sometimes I shove into them on purpose as they walk along so slowly, not looking where they are going. They apologise, assuming it's their fault because they know they are not looking. It's a small joy.

Sometimes I want to avoid the rush hour entirely. As neither Jones nor I have anyone waiting at home, we might stop for a drink or a meal to bypass being squashed by the multitudes going home to their families. Perhaps we are simply prolonging the feeling of walking into our empty apartments. I suspect that's how Jones feels, but for me arriving home is always a welcome relief from the forced social interacting that my workday demands.

As the SkyCar slows to a stop, we quickly push to the front of the crowded carriage.

We glance at each other as the doors slide open and then look no more. I move quickly and with focus, immediately losing sight of Jones. He might as well be dead to me or never have existed. It's just me and the crowd. I push, I shove and shoulder my way through. I sidestep, I weave, I dodge. If I had to, I'd leap. I take the stairs, for fitness and for speed. It's a long way down but it's faster than the travellator or the lift, with only a few of us in the stair well. I skip three, sometimes four steps at a time with my extended stride. Soon I'm on the street. It's only two blocks to my office, but there are obstacles. I'm ever watchful, keeping an eye on the horizon for potential hurdles and glancing to the footpath to ensure I'm not tripped up by potholes or other pitfalls. I move from the footpath to the street if I must. Avoiding AutoElectrics, buses, trams and incessant hovering delivery drones. I'm nimble. I'm gone before they see me. In the back of my mind, I know Jones is doing the same thing and another hundred like him from my office alone. How many hundreds or more are doing what we are doing to get to their treasured hot desks? To play their part, to further the work of The Collective.

I see some flashing orange lights ahead. I notice the back of Jones' head a few meters in front of me. There's a holdup and the crowd of office workers, pushing to get in on time, is grinding to a halt. Jones is caught and can't go forward or back. I see a side street and quickly move out of the crowd before the wave of stagnation reaches me. A bot whizzes by my ear, annoying but a good indicator that I'm taking a faster route. It's a longer way around, but I'll get to the office ahead of everyone caught by the stop in pedestrian traffic. Jones will be pissed, and envious.

I emerge from the side street and see the holdup behind. Two AutoElectrics smashed into each other blocking the small inner-city street and a couple of cops struggling to hold back the pedestrian hordes. They are pushing and pulsating at the edges of the cordon and it won't be long before they spill over. I keep moving, knowing there are only moments before the cops clear the road. It's that or face a riot of angry office workers.

I reach my building and the full joy of the street holdup washes over me as I take the lift alone to my floor. I'm well ahead of everyone, but that's no reason to rest on my laurels. I must keep focus until that desk is mine.

The lift doors open. My swipe card in hand, I glide quickly through the doors and weave through the sea of desks, my eyes on the prize. There it is, my desk by the window. Tucked in the corner, nothing on it. The floor is empty as far as I can see, and I safely slide myself on to the chair and put my bag on top of the table to claim my prize. I sit a moment and scan the empty office. A few bodies trickle in. I look for Jones but he's not amongst them. Likely still caught in the pedestrian hold-up on the street or the impending morning queue for the lift. I pull my laptop from my bag and quickly set up my desk for the day's work ahead. Walking briskly to the other corner of the office I find Jones' preferred hot desk still empty and place my coat on the chair. I retrieve a book and glasses case from my bag, a pen and notepad and place them on the desk to ensure it looks occupied. Jones will know they are mine and return them gratefully at meal break.

Returning to my hot desk, I open my laptop and assess the daily deadlines. A bunch of pre-count second-hand reallocations, some fine issuance for non-compliance of Notice to Downsize. Achievable if I start soon. Pre-Count week is always busy, but not as crazy as post-count when all the data flows in and we drown in rectifications and forced compliance.

The office is filling up. The roadblock and the lift queues will be cleared soon. The talkers will be amongst the last to make the floor. The inevitable conversations about the impending count. Jones will fill me in on the morning delays at meal break. I look out the window a moment. Content in having secured my spot, I almost smile, knowing Jones will be pleased to have his. I put in my earbuds, turn up the volume, take a breath and tune my mind to work. Only three days to 'The Counting' but I can't let that shift my focus.

I feel a hand on my shoulder and look up from my laptop. It's Jones.

'Meal break,' he says. 'You didn't hear the chimes?'

I pull out my earbuds.

'Oh,' he says. 'Are you breaking?'

'Yes. Let's go,' I reply.

We join the cafeteria line and shuffle along.

'Thanks for getting my desk,' Jones says. 'I really got jammed this morning. I thought I was way ahead of you.'

'You were until the hold-up. I was lucky, got to the side street before the backup. Had to take a full circle but since everyone else was locked in between 5th and 4th it didn't matter.'

We reach the hot food. 'Can I have the plant-based meat loaf and roast vegetables, thanks,' Jones orders. 'And a milk-like piccolo.'

'Same, thank you,' I say, 'but make my coffee a flat milk-like white.'

'Since when did you have milk-like?' Jones asks.

'Since they stopped getting the good soy. Plus, I'm counting the calories just now.' I pat my small but none the less protruding belly.

'Aren't we all,' says Jones.

'Extra points for keeping to my BMI.' Jones leaves my comment hanging. I know he's struggling to keep under his weight quota.

We take a seat in the middle of the cafeteria, content to sit anywhere and let the hot-deskers that got shitty spots for the day at least have a window seat for meal break.

'So, The Count,' Jones says as he tucks into his fake-meat meatloaf.

'The Count,' I say.

'What's your master plan then this year?' he asks. We both know what he's asking. The Counting lasts a week, but the sooner you finish the more time you can have to do nothing. We all want to do our bit for The Collective. We all want to be under our quota. But more than that we want to get our count done quickly so we can have that precious free time. That post-count time where everything we own is recorded and compared to what we had last year. Where we are rewarded for not having any new things. Where we are praised for only replacing something that has legitimately broken. That our overall collection of goods is the same or lower than the year before. But to reach post-count ahead of the timeline, well that is like some kind of alchemy. It's time off the clock. It's time to do whatever you want in an unaccounted way.

'I heard that Williams did his count last year in two days.' Jones says. 'I mean it's easy for the minimalists. They have an unfair advantage. But Williams has two kids. How do you finish counting in two days with all that stuff kids collect?'

'Maybe the kids helped count?' I offered.

'Maybe. But what I heard was that he loaded up his parents' place with his stuff and left it in their garage. They didn't even know. Imagine if 'they' found out. The penalties!'

'It's not worth it Jones.' I say, knowing he's sounding me out. Asking if I think he can get away with what Williams may or may not have done. I don't even know Williams. Probably a made-up person. Jones is fishing for dangerous advice.

'Imagine though. All those boxes of things just left unaccounted. The time he saved.'

'It might seem like time saved, but it could turn into time served. If you know about it then someone else knows about it. People talk,' I say. 'What happened to Williams, whoever he is, anyway?'

'I don't know,' says Jones. 'He's a friend of a friend of my sister's.'

'Probably busted and then they would have called in the Cleaners at exorbitant rates. You do know what they do to people that fix the count, don't you Jones?'

'Of course, I do. He'd probably get 5 to 10,' Jones says.

'If he was lucky. Just imagine 5 to 10 years where you can't buy anything new. Even if something breaks. Even if you find someone to take your second-hand goods, you can't replace them. Just do the count Jones. You know it's good for you.'

'Of course, I'm doing the count!' Jones replies, his tone confirming I'm right, he's been contemplating Williams' plan.

I take a sip of my milk-like coffee and wince. 'To answer your first question, I'm all organized for my count. I have a system and plan a steady approach. I'll be done by Thursday so that will give me three days off. It's enough.'

'You're lucky,' Jones says. 'All you do is plan things. It's not in my nature to plan. I'm just a drone.'

'I'll email you my system, Jones. Just follow it and you'll be done in no time. Even my 89-year-old Aunt Caroline uses it and she's pre-tech. 'Got to get back,' I say and get to my feet.

'Me too,' Jones follows.

I abandon the rest of my milk-like flat white into the recycled liquids receptacle and place my tray on the 'returns' conveyor belt. It disappears through a hole in the wall and I wonder if it's people or robots that deal with my dirty dishes on the other side of the wall.

I wake early on the first day of the count. I collect vegetables from the fridge and place them on the bench and switch on the kitchen wall screen. I flick through live feeds until I find a calming bush scene. A watermark in the lower left corner tells me it's a live cam and I realise it's a little over an hour away. How long has it been since I've gone out to the bush and not just watched it on the telescreen? So long I wonder if it's real. I remember Caroline taking me as a child. We'd trudge along tracks in all kinds of weather. Hardly speaking. Occasionally she'd whisper something in my ear but just what her words were eludes me. Lost in the past I've worked to bury. Only minimalists and quick counters are allowed walks in the wilderness. Maybe I can get there if I work harder than I planned.

The sounds of the bush echo through my empty apartment. Bird song, twigs cracking, the gentle wind rustling through the leaves. The desire to be there is suddenly over-whelming. My built-up environment has me caged in by brick, mortar and steel, but also, I realise, by process. The commitment to said and unsaid rules completely structures my view. They are all that stand between me being at that scene now projected on the kitchen wall screen. It's beautiful the way the screen seamlessly covers the entire wall and makes it feel like I'm there. But I'm not there. And that feels ugly. All the walls in my apartment are the same, they can all tell me the same lie. They can all show me live feeds to places that I can't visit.

I close my eyes and in the darkness images of the trees rustling in the wind dance across my imagination. A sadness washes over me, the understanding that I can't simply get up and go there. The unseen restraints holding me in my place.

I open my eyes, take a knife from the block and make quick work of the vegetables. I transfer everything into the slow cooker, add stock, cover and dial it up to high. This meal will hold me for a few days, but the idea of finishing the count quickly and standing where that live cam is telecasting from has taken shape in my head. I take a deep breath and fill my lungs with determination.

I empty each cupboard one at a time onto the kitchen bench. I count and record each item as I return it to its place. If I find food that is out of date, or an object that is beyond its use, if I can't justify why I own it, then whatever it is gets placed in the waste or recycle bins. If it can be second-handed then there is a separate receptacle for that. My judgement is swift. My sorting containers are all within reach of where I'm working. They hardly fill as I've got next to nothing. I only keep what I need. Two of everything, just in case I have a friend over for dinner. I stop a moment and wonder if I'll ever bother having anyone over again. It would be easier if I just had one mug, one glass, one bowl, one plate, one knife, one fork, one spoon. Without thinking any further on it I take the second of each item and place them in the second-hand container. Better they are used or recycled than sitting unused in my kitchen cupboards, unnecessarily burdening my count.

The light is changing across the trees being beamed into my kitchen on the telescreen. I'm grateful I don't have to count the walls that double as screens. A legal loophole for pre-fab apartments that have them built-in during construction. The light dances across the bark, across the leaves. I need to be there. The count is helping me. I feel lighter having less and less each time I count.

The kitchen is done faster than I planned. The idea that when this is all over, I will have time to myself, time to hire an AutoElectric and get myself to that spot in the bush and not just hear and see but feel the wind, is becoming all consuming.

The phone rings and I see it's Aunt Caroline. I pause a second before answering. I could lose an hour on the phone with her if I'm not careful. I want to help her, but I also want to work fast.

'Aunt Caroline,' I answer, being careful not to ask 'how are you' lest I get a long reply.

'Nephew,' she says affectionately. 'I've got a stiff neck. Woke up with it this morning. Hardly done any counting.'

'Don't worry, Aunty. You have all week, and don't they have extra counters there to help you in the home?'

'It's not a home. It's assisted living.'

'Don't' they have assisted counting?'

'Yes, they do, I'm not worried about this stupid counting business. They can count my old ass for all I care.'

'I'm sorry about your neck,' I say, starting to get worried about the time I'm on the call. 'Was there something you wanted to ask me?' I venture, hoping to bring the conversation to a head.

'That's the thing, I don't think I do. I can't remember why I called you. I thought if I called you then you would help me remember what it was that I couldn't remember.'

'Why don't you just go and do something nice and relaxing now. It will come to you when you least expect it and you can message me.'

'Good idea. You know you're a good man. Better than my ratbag son.'

'You don't have a son,' I say.

'No but I dreamt I did, and he was a ratbag. Bye then,' she says and hangs up.

'Goodbye,' I say into the dial tone.

I set the phone to 'Do not disturb', something I should have done before I started. I move on to the bathroom. An easy win now will steel me for harder tasks ahead, and the bathroom is easy.

I've run down my stores in the lead-up. One toothpaste tube with just enough left in it to see me to the other end of the count. One electric toothbrush. No replacement heads. Like many things they will be automatically ordered the day after the count. One liquid hand soap dispenser, refillable of course, four rolls of toilet paper, hardly excessive. One razor, no refills (on order), one hand towel, one bath towel, one bathmat, combined shampoo, conditioner and body wash.

With the kitchen and bathroom both done today I could easily stop now and enjoy a few hours break or even pick it up tomorrow. I could eat my soup from the slow cooker, read or watch the main telescreen. But I'm ahead now so I might as well stay that way. I move to the hall cupboard.

Normally this part would stress me out, but I took precautions. A pre-count clean-out means I only have the essentials now. On the eye level shelf, one set of spare sheets for summer, one set of flannel sheets for winter, one blanket. The shelf above my spare towels, one bath towel, one tea towel, one hand towel. The top has one cleaning cloth and one spray container of all-purpose cleaner but is otherwise empty. The bottom space holds my vacuum cleaner and all its attachments neatly stored on a holder attached to the main handle. It's counted as one item.

Using my count data from last year I confirm all the items I own in my living room. Flat screen, sound system, coffee table, lounge. Nothing has changed, making this part of the count fast. I turn a few times to keep my eye on the changing light on the trees. It's afternoon. The day is going faster, though I know that's not real, just my perception of time. I make a quick departure by counting the rest of my furniture and belongings on display. My bed, bedside table, one artwork above my bed, a print of Klimt's 'Kiss'. One artwork in the lounge room, Dali 'The Persistence of Memory'. Do I still need them? I could remove them and just use the telescreens. One wall in each room is a screen. They can bring me images from all over the world. 'Kiss' reminds me of what I don't have. I don't kiss. I live alone. It's easier. I've chosen a non-kissing life. Sometimes I look at the painting and think it would be nice to kiss someone and other times I look at it and think of all the things that go with kissing. It's never just the kiss on its own. I imagine bubbles of items popping up around the kiss. All that goes with a relationship. Sure, there are benefits. Companionship, conversation, sex and a dual count concession. But on balance the single supplement is greater in my calculations. The kiss can bring time commitments, it can bring offspring and all their 'stuff'. It can bring expenses like dinner out, movies, theatre tickets, concerts. It's never just the kiss on its own.

I decide to keep the picture. I'm well under my quota.

The phone rings. It's Aunt Caroline again, but I let it go to VM. The phone rings again. It's Jones. He should know better than to call me in the count. It's sacred. He might as well call me on All Observance Day when I'm deep in TransMed. I ignore it.

The sun has set on the trees now and I turn off the kitchen wall screen. I've earned a rest. Only two rooms to go and although they are my most challenging, I can see that I'll finish a good 5 days ahead. A personal best and likely to win me some credits, kudos and water cooler chatter. Time for sleep so I can make an early start. Perhaps I'll really get to stand in that bushland before the week is out?

❁

I wake early. For a few moments I'm not sure what day it is. There's little light coming in through the windows. It must be somewhere between five and six am. I remember I'm in the count. The thought that I might finish today and be free from it pulls me from the bed. I'm already counting in my head. As I pull the sheets up and make my bed, I'm recording everything that I see. My sheets, the bedside table and lamp, the glass of water. I retrieve my phone from the kitchen table and return to my bedroom. I add everything that's pushing to get out of my head into the count reporting app. But I'm not truly ready to start. I've not done my TransMed, I've not eaten, I've not checked my phone. The count has taken over. A mix between the desire to finish with legendary status and a need to purge myself of belongings is rushing through me. I slide open the mirror door of my built-in wardrobe. This is the thorn in my side, this is where I will succeed or fail. This is the moment I've been both avoiding and working towards. The law on the count has some vagaries, but on this it is clear. All citizens must pour out the contents of their cupboards and wardrobes and return only those items that are of use.

A frenzy takes hold as I pull all my clothes out and place them on the bed. All my shirts, casual, business, formal. All my trousers. My one and only suit, worn last 3 years ago to a coupling. Jane and Elisa. They met in the office and seem very happy. I don't expect I'll need the suit for their uncoupling. I don't think they will have one. I won't need it for my own coupling. I don't intend to have one. I like the solitude of my life. I glance at Klimt's 'Kiss' and feel reassured again. Still I need to keep the suit for the unexpected. If it fits, it's okay to keep, if not I can second-hand it and buy a new one when and only when I need to. I pull on the jacket and it's fine. I'm so well within my BMI that it will probably never need to be replaced.

I pull out all my underwear, socks, t-shirts and gym gear and the pile grows on the bed. I pull down all my winter clothes. It's a mountain of garments that somehow form my means of expression. They tell the world something about me when I wear them.

I examine each item, log and return it to its place. If it's too worn, I put it in a separate pile for recycle or second-handing. The catharsis of the count is beginning to affect me. This is what the Collective wants. It wants me to see all that I own and see everything for what it is. I resist. I've always resisted. I've always just done the count, without feeling. It's the law and I follow the law. But the Collective wants more than that. They want the process to change me.

The more I look at each piece of clothing I own the less I want it. The second-hand pile grows, the number of items returning to the wardrobe shrinks.

I go to the kitchen to get more storage bags and notice my phone buzzing on the benchtop. Aunt Caroline again. I Ignore it. And three missed calls from Jones.

'Really Jones?' I say out loud, bemused. 'How hard is it to follow the count?' I slide the phone gently along the bench so it's out of my reach and turn on the wall screen. The light from the sunrise filters through the trees. The orange glow is like fire across the barky skin of the gum trees. I take a breath and the sight of it washes over me like an hour of TransMed.

I'm not sure how much time has passed, but I sit on the end of my bed and look at the open wardrobe now that I've finished. Bags of clothes line the wall under the window. I've never had my items down to so few.

I'm feeling the count flowing through my veins. Every breath fills me with more now that I have less. I sit with it, marvel at it. Then the image of my final hurdle comes to mind. One room remains, my true Achilles heel.

I line the hallway with my bags. It takes two trips down to the basement to load them into the second-hand pickup skip. Tossing the final bag feels like a great load has lifted.

I see the freedom it gives me float through the air, unseen, yet tangible. There is no-one around. It will be days before others in the building reach this stage. Walking to my garage I'm filled with both excitement and dread. I've come so far, removed so much. Can I keep the momentum going? Can I clear out that storage cabinet that sits at the back of my otherwise empty garage. I stand in front of the biometric reader. As it scans my face I wonder if it can detect my change in mood. My sense of floating like air, traversing existence like a ghost now that there is less connecting me to the physical world. How can it read me when I'm just particles of air? The garage opens. I must still be solid.

And there it sits. That tall and solitary figure. That container of my past, that holder of my history. I open the doors and it's almost empty. Other than one storage container that's wrapped in an old dusty blanket. I pull it from the wardrobe, unwrap the blanket and toss it to the side.

I've always counted it. I've always logged it as one item. 'Storage container – photos and letters'. It's never been picked up, but one day I could get audited. They could ask me to catalogue them all. They could ask me to specify what letters, what photos and how many. I'm tempted in this current mood of weightlessness to empty the contents straight into the one of the bins waiting patiently in the common garbage room. But I can't. This is my family now. Other than the one living remnant, Aunt Caroline. This is my childhood, my parents' lives. I've narrowed them down and down till all that was left sits here in this box. I can't throw it out. I've lived so long without them, but for as long as this box has been here, I've had them with me. Lost to me in an accident so long ago. A summer of exploration and adventure for them while I was off on my own adventure.

I take the container out of the wardrobe and put it to one side of the otherwise empty garage. If I can clear the garage, then the space can be rented. Those with too much can pay the price of having somewhere to hold it.

I lay out the dusty old blanket and flip the wardrobe onto it. Pulling the ends, I drag it to the rubbish room. I flip it upright into the collection zone and toss the blanket into the recycle clothes bin.

Back in my garage I empty the contents of the box onto the floor. It's dusty but I don't care. I photograph everything with my phone. I move quickly and accurately. I don't want to get bogged down in memory. I don't want to feel that moment when my friend's mother pulled me aside from our antics in their backyard pool to tell me there had been a car accident. Goosebumps on my wet skin from the cool air and a shudder of harsh reality delivered with softly spoken words into my child's ear. Shattering my world like a rock through a glass window. I don't want to be pulled back into that moment when Aunt Caroline came to collect me. Tearing me away from my summer holiday to the coldness of loss. From swimming, running and riding, to sitting at a funeral and then hours and days in my empty house while my aunt arranged everything. I never understood why she didn't just leave me with my friend and his family, where I was warm and happy.

I snap each photo and it's logged and documented in the Collective's count app and the pain of it is almost gone. I return everything to the box, close my garage door and toss the box into the bin. It's a strange feeling. I'm almost tempted to delete the digital files I've just made but for now the sense of letting go by throwing the 'real' items is enough. I've tossed my feelings of loss and longing away with that box and all it holds. I imagine it being crushed and decimated in a garbage press. Fragmented and torn into pieces that can never be reconstructed. I don't need it anymore. I don't need those feelings. I just need the strength that experiencing them gave me.

When I return to my apartment the phone is buzzing. It's Jones. I've got nothing left to sort out so I might as well answer.

'What Jones?' I say.

'I think they are onto me,' he says.

'I have no idea what you're talking about,' I say, aware he's probably being tapped, but also because I have no idea what he's talking about.

'My in-laws,' he says.

'Still, you are not making any sense Jones. If you've done something wrong then sort it out, but for the Collective's sake don't tell me about it unless you want it reported.'

'I haven't done anything,' he says unconvincingly. 'But you wouldn't report me, would you? You're my friend,' he says.

'I am your friend, but I'm also a citizen of the Collective, and like you, a government employee!' I'm trying to tell him to shut the fuck up as best I can without implicating myself in any way, shape or form.

'I just got back from my in-laws,' he says. And now I know exactly what he's done.

He hates his in-laws. He does everything to avoid his in-laws. He'd drive a thousand clicks in an AutoElectric on surge pricing in the opposite direction to avoid his in-laws. After his wife died, he never wanted to see them again. But he's gone and done it. He's put unaccounted stuff in their house. What could he have that was so terrible to count that he felt he had to hide it?

'Visit them again tomorrow and be nice to them,' I suggest, hoping he gets my meaning that he should go back ASAP and take his stuff back. 'You shouldn't be travelling in the count. But if you must see them again, then do it quickly and get on with it, Jones. It's not that hard.'

'It's everything,' he says. 'It's Elisabeth.'

'Pull it together, Jones.' He's really losing it. It must be a hoard of his wife's belongings. And unlike me and my past, Jones is not willing or able at this stage to let it go. He's probably never counted all that stuff. And who knows what he has done with it every year since her death. Perhaps he has just ignored it and is finally realizing an audit could come with any count. You don't want a bureau person watching you do the count and finding a bunch of things you've never reported.

'Can I come over?' he says.

'No, Jones.' Not in the count. 'Have you gone mad?'

'No, I'm fine. Of course. It was unfair of me to ask. You are right. I'll visit them tomorrow. See you on Monday,' he rings off.

I take a deep breath. Jones is up to his ears. He'll be caught for sure just based on that call. And they will drag me in for questioning. I go over the call in my mind. There's nothing they can pin me on. In fact, they will probably have to give me some sort of award for compliance.

I want to enjoy my moment of letting everything go. I want to plan my visit tomorrow to the forest that I've been watching on my kitchen wall. Easy enough. The location is all there. Simply press a few buttons and the AutoElectric will come when booked. I start the process and I'm surprised its only ninety minutes away. I book it, make myself a cup of coffee and sit back and enjoy watching the trees in the light breeze knowing I will be standing there tomorrow. I plan a simple meal to take. Sandwiches and a thermos of coffee.

The phone buzzes again. It's Aunt Caroline.

'Aunty, everything ok? You know it's the Count don't you?'

'Hello, this number is the emergency contact for Caroline Watson.'

'Yes?'

'I'm afraid her life signs have ceased. As next of kin you are required to attend her property as soon as possible and conclude her count.'

'But where is she?'

'Don't worry about that, her remains are being treated respectfully. You can visit at the HumanCompost site after concluding her personal affairs. You have 3 days. You can apply for an extension of 3 days as this has occurred during the count. We are not unreasonable.' They hang up.

The light in the forest darkens as a cloud passes over. My sense of letting go, my desire to be somewhere else, somewhere simpler is as transient as the light appearing and disappearing from the surface of the trees.

I change my AutoElectric booking to Caroline's residence and set for ASAP pickup. A TransMed awareness slips over me as I stare at the trees and the overlay map tracking the arrival of my AutoElectric. I breath steadily, the chaos of Aunt Caroline's affairs pushing at the edges of my calm. I want to observe and not react, but I feel it rising.

The car arrives quickly. It's a short ride to Caroline's. The biometric scan allows me in. It's already transferred to me. There is no sign of Caroline, or the collection team. I walk through the assisted living estate to her townhouse. I enter and I'm immediately hit by the smell of dust. There are items everywhere. She'd clearly started her count but in a haphazard and chaotic way. I go to each room. Her bedroom built-in is half filled with stuff and half emptied into the room. So much stuff. She could not have been reporting all of it. It's too much for one person to own. Perhaps she really didn't care about the law. She always told me she complied, but then always indignant about it. She'd kept her hoarding well hidden in her wardrobes. My phone buzzes. It's a message from the Collective. Caroline's previous count is now attached to my quota, detailed in my app. I open it. She's been a chronic under reporter. But now that someone else has been here they will be onto it. I have no choice. Either it all goes, or I spend the rest of the count sorting.

I sit on the lounge and look out the window into her small courtyard. I notice a cup of tea spilled on the floor. I must be sitting where she died, the end of her life signs triggering an alarm. I imagine the room filling with the retrieval team. The horror on their faces. Not from the dead body, but from all the stuff that's been turned out of the wardrobes. All my Aunt's possessions sprawled out mid-count. She had no intention of reporting it all. A last act of defiance. A 'fuck-you' to the collective. A mess for them to clean up. But it's my mess now. It's all on my quota and I don't want it. I want that moment in the bush. I want to sit free of the count.

I lift my phone to my face to unlock it and order an emergency count clean-up team. It will cost a bomb, an up-front fee plus 20% of any resale of second-handed goods. I figure I can take it out of whatever Aunt Caroline has left me. But I really don't care about the money. I just want to get out. I don't want the burden of her possessions on my account, on my mind, on me.

I wait for the clean-up team to arrive and stare at the tea stain on the floor. The last action of a dying woman. Soon this room will be empty and there will be nothing but my memory of her. Perhaps a small collection of digital assets, but everything tangible she owned will be dispersed, recycled or destroyed. I can't look at the stain any longer. I can't sit in this spot, wondering if she felt pain, regret or loneliness in her last moments.

The door chime rings and I jump to my feet. I buzz in the clean-up team. A fortyish woman and two young men in overalls. They look like twins. She nods at them and they wander off, assessing the workload. The disdain in their eye, in their demeanour is palpable.

'You want the total package?' the boss lady says to me. 'Clean out, resale where possible, profit share?'

'Yes,' I say.

She holds her phone up to my face. 'Biometric approval.'

'Of course,' I say and then hold myself still for the scan.

'We'll get to work.' She calls over her two young assistants, speaks softly to them and they get to work. One raises an eyebrow at me. A faint look of understanding. He'd like to be elsewhere too.

The ride is smooth. The roads are empty. Everyone is in the middle of the Count. The further away from the city the calmer I feel. I see fewer and fewer houses. Each one holding people, doing their counting. Sorting their stuff.

The AutoElectric pulls into an empty car park and the destination is transferred back to my phone. As soon as I'm clear of the AutoElectric it reverses and drives off. I probably should have held it, but I don't know how long I'll be, and I don't care. I follow the path, my phone telling me that I'm getting closer to the feed point, to where the camera sits that sends its images and sound into my kitchen. It's off the main track a little but I'm not concerned. A thin trail, trees overhanging and eucalyptus scented air filling my lungs. Clearing out the dusty remnants lingering from my Aunt's townhouse. I reach a clearing. I see the camera sitting on top of a poll about my height, housed in all-weather casing. A sign mounted under it at eye level, 'Do Not Disturb – Live Streaming in Progress – Penalties Apply'. I have no wish to interrupt those watching at home, those souls in the middle of their counts that, not unlike me, are placated by the sound and sight of the bush on their wall screens.

I notice a large flat rock a few metres back and gently step my way towards it, conscious not to make any unnatural sounds, nothing that could give away the presence of a human being. I sit on the rock and take in the scene. The air, the cool crisp air. I'm tempted to TransMed but I don't want to close my eyes. I want to immerse myself in this moment, with all my senses. The soft sounds fill my ears, clicks and cracks of the bush, the call of a whipbird. It holds me. It's real in a way nothing else in my life is real. The bush asks nothing of me and I ask nothing of it other than for it to go about its business, for it to follow its own rules of nature that do not apply to the decrees of The Collective, or to any laws that humans have ever dared to set down for it. Try as they might they can control our lives with rules and regulations, but they can't get nature to obey. They can only destroy it or allow it to be.

I think about Jones, suffering under the system. Not seeing how to exist outside of it. And then Caroline. My last remaining relative. Her townhouse full of burdensome stuff, being sorted and deconstructed by three strangers she'd never met. I shake it off, feeling grateful she took me in. Seeing the mistakes she made, but knowing she did her best. She was so very unprepared to be a parent. The task thrust upon her, much as her life belongings were now thrust upon me. But they are just objects. It's all just stuff and it means nothing to me now. Nothing but a transient blip on nature's radar. This is where I will be when they come for me.

I'd gladly trade all I have, as long as they let me sit here from time to time and watch in fascination as real life unfolds.

The light changes. The warm orange glow of the sun caressing the trees. The wind moving gently through the leaves.

My phone buzzes with a message. A text from Caroline. I read in wonder as she speaks to me, as if from the other side of this existence.

'I am gone now and have only this to share. All else you can give away or sell. You've probably already called in the cleaners. I would. When you were a boy, I took you out for walks in the bush. Not just because I didn't know what else to do with you but because in the silence we didn't need to speak. Nature didn't care about our problems and so we could lose ourselves there. Remember what I used to say?

'Listening to the sound of the wind through the trees can both break and mend the human heart. My hope for you is that it mends.'

I close my eyes and listen and realise for the first time since those words of loss were whispered in my ears, that I am smiling. Smiling ear to ear, like the boy I was. The boy lost in the joy of summer before the winter took the warmth away.

Finish

Prelude

One hundred and fifty million kilometres away from the Earth a big ball of fire busily burns away, converting four hundred million tons of hydrogen into helium every second in a seemingly endless nuclear fusion.

As our world orbits the Sun, we revolve our lives around our own daily concerns, forgetting that the big bright light in the sky, by its very nature, creates our day and feeds our existence. Eight minutes after its atomic birth the light that reaches Earth helps plants photosynthesise, taking in carbon dioxide and releasing oxygen.

Buried by our needs, our hopes, our dreams, our petty dislikes, our great loves and our monstrous hates, is a forgotten truth. It is so intrinsically human that we are capable of pushing this thought to the dark reaches of our primitive brains, that we know the words but don't truly appreciate the concept. We can tell ourselves what we like but there's no getting away from it. You can't hide from the truth forever, and this is true, so listen up.

Our lives are just a by-product of a cosmic breath!

Patrick closed his notebook, content with another great thought committed to paper. As he reclined into the comfort of his manager's plush office chair the feeling of self-satisfaction gave way to a pervasive self-doubt: how likely was it that a set of human eyes other than his own would ever read his words? His thoughts would remain just that, his own. To ensure that fate, he hastily removed the notebook from sight and shoved it into his bag. He shifted focus from the sense of his own mediocrity to that of his manager's. Leaning back further into the leather-padded chair he surveyed the room with contempt. Except for his position of authority, Patrick's manager was an inferior in every respect. The man's gruff manner, his constant barking of orders, ensured his control but alienated him from his subordinates. To Patrick he was a man to be managed. There were ways of dealing with him to get what you wanted: picking times when he was most distracted to ask for personal leave, never presenting him with an unsolved problem, always offering a solution no matter how stupid it may seem. Like a dog gnawing into a bone your offering would be viciously snatched and ripped into pieces, devoured before your eyes and the remnants spat back at your feet. But he would be secretly grateful you threw him something to sink his teeth into. Yes, he was to be managed and by no means trusted. A company man through and through, a company man who had access to information being withheld from Patrick. He looked around the room again, attempting to intuit where his superior would hide things he didn't want his subordinates to find.

The office was dark other than the light emanating from the desk lamp and a few beams of orange glow that crept in around the edges of the block-out blind covering the large window on one side of the office. A glint of light reflecting on the stainless steel filing cabinet in the corner of the room pulled Patrick to his feet and drew him towards it.

The vivid orange light from outside was easing rapidly, receding as the day drew to a close. Another twilight gone, another twilight spent alone, the most precious part of the day nearly over and nothing but a long lonely night ahead. With the sun setting fast Patrick had to increase his pace if he didn't want his break and enter to be discovered, if he didn't want to waste having braved the intense heat of the sun to be in the office a few hours early. His colleagues would soon filter in, once the cover of night gave them safe passage. He stood at the locked cabinet and tugged ineffectually at the top drawer. Yes there was definitely something in here that was not meant for Patrick, making him all the more determined to gain access.

Back at the desk he pulled open drawers, turned over papers, lifted up objects. No key to be found, nothing. He spotted the coffee cup next to the keyboard. 'Let me drop everything and fix your problem' branded on it in large type. His manager would often sit behind his desk holding the cup at eye level while subordinates talked to him, not answering, just waiting for them to read the message, get the point and get out of his office. If they took too long to register he'd soon throw them out, barking at them as they retreated. In all the time Patrick had worked with the man he'd never actually seen him drink from it. The cup was just a prop, another object littering a cluttered desk. Patrick picked it up, raised it to his eye in the manner of his superior, fleshing out what it felt like to be such a dickhead, before tipping it over and pouring the key into his palm.

Patrick rummaged around the now unlocked filing cabinet drawer. A bottle of vodka, some retro porn magazines, there must be more the man was hiding. Then bingo, official looking documents – 'Project Helios' – it smelled clandestine. His eager fingers took hold of the report and he could feel its suppression itching to be released.

With the document in hand he quickly covered his tracks – easy enough given it was a mess when he'd arrived. Lock the cabinet, key back in the cup, papers back in their stacks. He scooped up his bag and hit a button on his manager's desk. The large block-out blinds rose allowing the last vibrant orange rays of the sunset to fill the room, removing all shapes and objects with its intense glare. Then as the sun dropped behind the horizon and the room crept into darkness, Patrick closed the office door behind him and moved quietly to his workstation.

Compared to his supervisor's office, Patrick's desk was uncluttered and sparse. He'd never given the space much thought, other than to avoid it. What was the point in decorating? It annoyed him the way his co-workers littered their spaces with photos of families and friends, displaying them as some measure of achievement. 'This is what I have outside of this place, what do you have?' Why should he offer a window into his life to be assessed and ranked amongst the workforce? Worse still were postings of platitudes and self-motivating mantras, stuck to people's cubicles to help them through the day. At least Patrick wrote his own and kept them in his notebook. He didn't force them into his co-workers' field of vision the way they foisted their banalities on him.

His standard-issue ergonomic chair took his weight but creaked and squeaked as he shifted to find a comfortable position. He placed the document on the desk and pulled the chair in closer, ready, a little excited even, to discover what form of administrative ineptitude middle management had planned: a restructure, job losses, productivity gains? What idiocy would they be imposing on the workforce next?

As he began to read he was overcome with an acute awareness of the moment. As the words worked their way through his cerebral cortex he became filled with the horror of their reality. This was no minor administrative report. Patrick was discovering a truth that put his own concept of 'Cosmic Breath' into the realm of the pathetic. This was not a moment to be treasured, not a moment to be loved, but as clear a moment as any in his life, a milestone, a point of reference that couldn't be erased now that it had made its mark and he realised that from this point on his life wouldn't be the same.

Patrick sat with his hands frozen on the document and watched as workers began to arrive, safe now under the cover of night. Safe from the very sun in the sky that burned their lives into being but a sun now too strong for them to be exposed to.

He didn't move, didn't respond to his co-workers' 'good evenings', didn't react when the phone rang, didn't even realise he was continuing to breathe. There was only himself, the document before him and what was happening to his mind now that the information had transferred from paper to grey matter, nothing else registered, nothing else could.

Without fully knowing why, he stood, took the document in one hand, his car keys in the other and began to move. As he made his way steadily towards the exit he passed the early starters - some of them he knew, others he didn't, some he liked, others annoyed him, but they all looked like ghosts to him now. This pounding idea forced into his head by that wretched document made them all look dead, their activities meaningless, anything they might have to say useless. The information was infecting him – a vile fast moving virus corrupting and consuming his system.

The night air gave little relief, the ground still hot from the day's saturation of sunlight, the heat rising and filling his lungs. Every breath made him light-headed. He reached his car – the auto cooling made the interior a welcome relief from the outside air, but it didn't bring him back, didn't stop the pounding urge to keep moving. He started the car, capitulating to the unknown force propelling him forward. With no sense of destination, only a need to move away from that moment, that ground zero moment, he drove onto the open road. His lone vehicle travelled in the opposite direction to the stream of headlights making their way to work, collectively illuminating one side of the road as his sole set of headlights moved freely, seemingly unencumbered.

READ MORE

www.evanshapiro.net/road-to-nowhere